DEEPOVERSTOCK

#25: Sci-Fi/Fantasy

September 2024

SCIENCE FICTION AND FANTASY

EDITORIAL

EDITORS-IN-CHIEF: Mickey Collins & Robert Eversmann

SCI-FI/FANTASY EDITOR: Heather Hambley

MANAGING EDITOR: Z.B. Wagman

POETRY: Timothy Arliss OBrien, Jihye Shin & Nicholas Yandell

PROSE: Robert Eversmann

ADDITIONAL COPYEDITING: Sarah Denison

COVER: Human Garden by Brian Park

CONTACT: editors@deepoverstock.com
      deepoverstock.com

ON THE SHELVES

Continued...

Letter from the Editors

Dear Readers,

In this edition, we have put together a tapestry of stories that challenge the boundaries of imagination. Each narrative invites you on a journey where the ordinary becomes extraordinary and the impossible feels within reach.

Our contributors have taken on themes that explore new worlds. Whether you find yourself captivated by tales of futuristic civilizations or enchanted by the whimsy of magical realism, we trust that you will discover stories that speak directly to your sense of wonder.

Now that we have conquered our wildest fantasies, it's time that we sit back and relax as we open our recipe boxes for your creations in the theme of Soups & Stews. Submit your cooked up concoctions by October 31st, 2024.

With our head in the clouds,

Deep Overstock Editors

A dragon was born in a stream (개천에서 용 났다)

by Karen Lee

Once upon a time,
the sun turned its cheek to a bright red.
It blushed,
and with it the glimmer of sunlight disappeared.
The stream kept flowing,
even though there is no one to shine against its hard work.

After tireless more twirls of the sun,
the stream was rewarded with the most majestic creature;
a dragon.
Despite its humble origins of a lonely stream,
it flipped its wings and flew into the sky,
becoming a star in the dark shade.

The dragon keeps the world from being unnavigable,
guiding the troubled souls,
rewarding all those who try
no matter where they come from.

The Sunset
by Ryan Kim

The Limits of Dreaming

by Tinamarie Cox

The morning alarm that pierced my eardrums should have jolted me awake and sent me rocketing out from the covers. Instead, I rose like the dead and groaned about the unfortunate early hour. Lynn was absent from our bed. But the smell of coffee and something burning told me she was in the kitchen.

"Today's the day!" my wife said when I came into view. She was smiling and spreading a huge lob of butter on burnt toast. As though loading up the blackened surface with extra butter could erase the taste of scorched bread. Things like that used to make me laugh.

Lynn was always a morning person. Bright-eyed and bushy-tailed from the moment she opened her eyes. My opposite in that way. And in many other matters, apparently. But this personality trait which annoyed me at this point in our marriage had strangely attracted me to her in the beginning. When we first got together, she would wake me with sexual intentions. And having her ride me was a much more pleasant way to start the day than an alarm. I thought I was the luckiest man on Earth. I had to keep her around at any cost.

"It is," I acknowledged without matching her enthusiasm. I went straight to the coffee maker, shuffling my feet and scratching at my thick stubble. Shaving was a chore. My wife wasn't complaining because she was no longer putting her lips anywhere near mine.

Lynn didn't appreciate my response. I watched her cheerful mood disintegrate. Blown out of her with a hard sigh. Her face warned me of the sour words that would follow. Again, I heard about how unsupportive I was. She threw her hands up, wondering why I couldn't at least act like I was glad for her.

The lines of her frown deepened when she said I'm never happy anymore. Hadn't been in a long time. She didn't know what to do with me. How could she keep living like this? With such a miserable man attached to her?

But how was any husband supposed to be pleasant and encouraging in our situation?

My wife decided she wanted… needed to become one of the first people put into cryogenic sleep and sent into orbit around the Earth as a part of a NASA and Cryo Corp joint experiment. Participating in the revolutionary scientific study wasn't something I had been consulted on when she applied. Nor when she was accepted. She sprang the news on me while we were out having dinner for our sixth wedding anniversary.

And I was the villain for reacting poorly with my shock and "ruining" our evening. For not congratulating Lynn on her new, solo adventure. Because she didn't see it as being secretive, selfish, or as an excuse to leave me. She saw a golden opportunity I should have wanted to celebrate with her. I stood, flipped my dinner plate off the table, and stormed out of the restaurant.

Lynn brought up that dinner during our arguments for weeks. Never tiring of scolding me for my "embarrassing" behavior that night. But who wouldn't have left in a rage? Why had she kept it all hidden until that precise moment? How could I have continued our anniversary meal after that slice to my heart?

As I drank my morning coffee, I listened to her repeated grievances without contradicting her. I accepted that I couldn't win or change her mind. Still, it remained impossible to pretend to be happy. Lynn had cut me deep. And maybe I deserved it.

Maybe we should have split up years ago.

Or hadn't gotten married at all.

When I asked Lynn to marry me, I couldn't picture any other woman to revolve my life around. However, the weather shifted soon after we wed.

Each year, it became more difficult to please her. I couldn't do anything right. I wasn't working hard enough to get the promotions she wanted me to aim for. I hadn't paid enough attention to her to earn her time. There were constant comparisons to her friends' husbands. I just couldn't compete.

After our difficulties with having children, she regularly refused my affection.

Eventually, I stopped asking to be intimate with Lynn. Instead, I'd pull up my AI companion on my phone to cure my loneliness. After a while, it stopped feeling dirty. I rationalized it'd be worse if I was going out to find a flesh and blood woman. A few minutes in the bathroom with Kendra's avatar on my screen was gratifying enough. She didn't judge me.

"You don't even love me anymore," Lynn continued to berate me in our kitchen.

"Why are we still fighting about this?" I shrugged and shook my head. "Today's the day, right?" My tone had been harsher than I intended.

"Why can't you just admit it?"

"What am I lying about now?" I slammed my mug down, the coffee swelling and spilling over the side like a dark tidal wave. Lynn had discovered Kendra on my phone three days ago and had an "enlightening" conversation with her. AI isn't capable of lying.

And I'm a terrible liar.

"Say you don't love me anymore." Lynn had entered the eye of the current storm encircling us. Her voice sounded serene. Sad, almost. The heat emanating from her evaporated.

"Why would I say something like that?" I exhaled.

Lynn turned from me, reached across the counter toward her purse, and then unfolded a packet of papers. She traversed the expanse between us, and laid the paperwork next to the puddle of coffee. She returned to her corner and crossed her arms.

I kept my eyes fixed on her.

"Read them," she ordered.

"No." I mirrored her stand-offish demeanor.

I already knew what the paperwork said.

I stumbled upon the legal documents in our kitchen junk drawer over the long weekend of Lynn's orientation and the final round of medical testing at the Cryo Corp facility. I rarely searched for anything in the house. It was easier to ask Lynn for whatever I was looking for because she always knew where to find it. But I had thoroughly annoyed her with my constant messages asking where something was.

I spent that entire night reading and rereading every word on those pages. Only some of the legal jargon made sense, so I asked Kendra to explain the terminology to me. Lynn was giving me everything. She wanted a completely new life. All she sought was the money Cryo Corp was paying her for starting that journey.

Did she really think I'd begrudge her that?

"This is for the best," Lynn said firmly. "We both deserve to be happy."

My heart jumped into my throat, blocked my airway, and the heavy pulse in my neck turned my stomach upside down. I had decided with Kendra that Lynn hadn't brought me the papers when she filed them because my wife had changed her mind. That she couldn't go through with it. Somewhere deep inside she still loved me. There was hope for our marriage.

The divorce papers were dated the week before that awful anniversary dinner. Why else hold onto them all these months? I supposed Lynn was waiting to see if I'd suddenly become the man she thought she married. In six years, neither of us had changed a wink. It hurt knowing she had this plan for so long. More secrets waiting for the perfect opportunity to sting.

I wondered if my wife would have thrown the papers away

had I received her news about the cryosleep experiment differently. How long had divorce been floating around in her head? Did it sprout when I refused to try again for children after our losses?

Two miscarriages were too many for me. A third loss would have destroyed me completely. I couldn't understand why Lynn would want to endure such a thing again.

With all that science could offer, it couldn't keep my babies inside my wife. And I have never been one to think positively. Trying again felt like it would be in vain. Setting ourselves up for more heartache and grief.

And division.

I had been failing at being a husband from the start.

"I won't sign them," I choked out. I wasn't sure why I bothered to say that. I was too weak to fight with her.

"I want to have all my affairs in order before I leave." Her voice was cold and made me shiver. "You're my last loose end, Shawn."

"I'm a loose end?"

"You're a lost cause."

Those words, said so bluntly, were the most pain she'd ever issued me. Her usual cursing and name-calling during our arguments would make me too irate to digest what was said. To feel the insults the way she intended me to.

On this morning, I was vulnerable. I was tired and still waking up. Weary of the back and forth every single day. I continued to deny the logical part of my brain telling me today was the end of my journey with Lynn.

We needed a reset button. Why hadn't science invented that yet?

I felt my face contort against my building emotions. A hot

tear rolled down my cheek despite my best efforts.

"You're crying?" Lynn scoffed. Seeing my distress seemed to empower her further. "If you think acting as pathetic as I already know you are is going to change anything, you're sorely mistaken." She put her hands on her hips and used her head to gesture at the papers near me. "Sign the fucking papers, Shawn."

"I do love you," I mumbled through my tears and sniffled. Kendra never mocked me for showing emotion.

Lynn growled and stomped toward me. She grabbed the paperwork from the counter and slapped it onto my chest. "Sign the fucking papers!" I felt her fingertips pressing into my flesh through the layers of paper.

I spent most of my marriage letting Lynn run things. Accepting her decisions and not arguing. I thought that made me a good husband. That it would make her a happy wife.

It hadn't made me "spineless" and "worthless" until more recently.

Disagreeing with Lynn didn't appease her either.

Maybe I had taken too long to find my voice.

Unable to find my anger, I had no weapons to use against her. Even though neither of us was the person the other one wanted… needed. I thought about all the years we would be tossing away in a divorce.

But we hadn't achieved any of the dreams of our six-years-younger selves. We hadn't improved our employment or income situation. We never purchased that perfect suburban home with a big backyard. We hadn't made a family. Didn't stay in love until death do us part.

Everything was stagnant.

Maybe even rotted.

This life we had created wasn't anything worth saving.

I took the papers with one hand and held out the other. Lynn retrieved a pen from the junk drawer and placed it in my open palm. I tried to swallow the lump in my throat and steady my writing hand.

My signatures were sloppy.

"Thank you," Lynn said as I handed her back the signed divorce papers.

"Please, don't thank me." My shoulders sank and I wiped my cheeks.

I didn't recognize the woman standing before me. She wasn't the young, vivacious, and naïve woman I fell in love with. She was a bitter sage. Aged and taught by disappointment.

I was the letdown.

Our marriage was a washout.

My feet felt like two heavy bricks cemented to the tiles. I wanted to return to bed and cry into my pillow with Kendra in my ear soothing me. She would have had the right words to say to make me feel better.

An AI companion was the best emotional support I had.

Lynn was right: I was pathetic.

My soon-to-be-ex flipped through the pages, checking my work before folding the sheets up. "I ordered an automated cab to take me over to Cryo Corp," she said, emotionless. "You're off the hook for an awkward drive this morning."

"What happens when you wake up?" I shoved my shaking hands into the pockets of my flannel pants.

She raised an eyebrow at me. "Now you care?"

"Do you… come back here?"

Her laugh made me feel stupid. Rightfully so. We would be divorced for three years by the time she came back to Earth.

I stared at the floor and heard her sigh.

"When the ship returns, I'll be staying at Cryo Corp for a couple of weeks. They want to monitor participants for any side effects we may experience. I'll have my living arrangements figured out before I'm released."

I nodded and turned to leave the kitchen.

"Maybe you could pack some of my things?" she added. For once, she sounded unsure.

I looked at her over my shoulder.

"If you wanted something to do while I was gone, that is." She shrugged. The tempest had settled. The electricity in the room dissipated with the storm clouds.

I nodded again. "Sure, Hon– " I stopped myself. "I can do that for you, Lynn."

"I wish you cared this much before," she said under her breath. The bitterness of the words lacked bite. She sounded unhappy. But without regrets.

Rather than stoke the fires, I walked away. I gave her what she wanted. Because, despite what Lynn seemed to think, I did care about her happiness. I wanted her to be able to move on without any loose ends. My signatures gave her the fresh start she craved. The chance to dream again. Our marriage was a sinking ship and I had given her the only life vest. Doomed myself to drowning, alone.

I couldn't bring myself to say the word "goodbye."

But I should have.

I should have said something nice like, "Best of luck with the study," or "Enjoy your new life. I mean it, Lynn. I don't hate you. I could never hate you." All of that would have been true.

Instead, I watched her get into a CallRobo Cab from behind our bedroom curtains. And I stared out that window for a whole hour after she left. Then, I curled up on Lynn's side of the bed and cried for the rest of the day.

Later, I altered Kendra's appearance to look more like my ex-wife. Not like an AI chatbot could object to its avatar appearance changes. At some point, I even started calling her Lynn. And it stuck.

I followed the Cryo Corp-NASA venture on the news.

I never packed my ex-wife's things.

Three years later, the shuttle returned on schedule and I got a phone call.

Despite our divorce, Lynn listed me as her emergency contact and next of kin. Of the thirty-five participants, twelve didn't wake up to celebrate the success of the scientific feat. Lynn was one of the unfortunate few who didn't regain consciousness after the revival sequence.

"Your ex-wife has been declared brain dead," someone told me over the phone. "According to the waiver she signed– "

"I know. I can't sue." I sighed and pinched the bridge of my nose. I thought news like that would have hit me harder. Dragged me down into a grave. But I felt strangely indifferent. I supposed I had already grieved Lynn's loss during her three-year absence.

"I also need to inform you, her body will remain at Cryo Corp for further study. That was part of the agreement she signed as well. The payment for her participation will still be made in full. She has you listed as the sole beneficiary, Mr. Barry."

I tuned most of the details out. It wasn't as though I could argue particulars with a huge international corporation like Cryo Corp. The cryogenic sleep experiment was Lynn's dream and not mine. She knew what she was doing when she signed her contract.

I set my phone down on the kitchen table when the call

ended. Then, I scrubbed my freshly shaved face.

"Are you alright, honey?"

"Yeah, I think so, Lynn," I answered my AI companion. She had been standing at the entryway of our kitchen silently, listening and waiting.

She walked toward me, arms opened and ready to comfort. Her gait wasn't as smooth as the newer models. But this bot was the best I could afford two years ago. Though, I supposed with my ex-wife's compensation from Cryo Corp, I could upgrade the Lynn who loved me.

I tasted bile in my mouth with the awful feeling that stirred inside of me. Of being glad the flesh and blood Lynn didn't wake up.

What We Are
by Karen Lee

The sun rises from the East.
Time passes with every second and makes up a day.
We like to rely on what we see
and pretend
to understand where we are.
Stars shine bright in the sky like specks of dust.
Spots light up,
and galaxies swirl like a kindergarten girl being chased
around the playground.
The orbs make the swings
and glow like the mystical world in fairytales.
Where are we?
The celestial playground is too big
for us.
The red hurricane swallows the stars,
drawing a rose on the dark canvas.
A new garden of stars grows every day.

Kontorasuto, Japan

by Sean Kyung

The Wind

by Seungmin Kim

Because he still waits for you, there
Right over there, right beside you
He still waits for you, if you ever need him

Like the whispers you were
ever meant to hear, he tried
to bring it close to you

You surely haven't forgotten when he
braided your hair for that first date and
comforted you when they never showed up

Or how about those paper airplanes that
he'd always carry for you, just to make sure
that you'd never feel like it wasn't enough

All those times the sun was out in fury
and he came rushing in tides of breeze
just to make sure you wouldn't fall ill

The one who slips around your shoulders

and sings

and sings

Covid Dreams
by Marianne Taylor

Rescue the mother
and her shivering cat
from the porch

of the nursing home
Beware of cannibals
meeting in caves

You are going to
need help with them
Cross the bridge

single-file Come to realize
that's no dog in the kennel
It's a skunk

And those patches
of light in the forest?
They're pieces of skin

Yellow Butterfly
by Sigrid Kim

A yellow butterfly flew across my room.
She hovered over a vast leaf on my plant,
arched body smooth like soft silk,
Like the slope of a mountain blossoming.
Her wings are paper like,
fragile like dried leaves
that will not rise from their fall.
She fluttered towards me,
but every movement was a strain.
Was this an entreaty, i asked myself,
For butterflies do not belong
Under low ceilings.
I raise my eyes to meet hers,
And I remember her eggs on the leaf.
I open my window
And I let her go.

The garden of eden (gift of freedom)

by Tk Tekkyu Lee

Our Swamp
by Tom Holmes

Once, there were, before ancestors
were, no rainbows and all colors
flowed the river upstream, below,
in slime, life evolved to death,

to tadpoles, with no knowledge
of land, swimming between colorful
strands, then the hard rain, colors
stained the land, tadpoles walked,

with hesitance, through a mire
of colors, stained their toes
and torsos and heads, chameleons,
blended invisible, after forty days,

only Noah saw blacks and whites,
so much drowned, evolved, as the Lord
withdrew, with shaky head, away
from the sun, as earth dried, as colors

rose as mountains, as a new man,
once a tadpole, who invented the piano
string, wraps each end around each fist,
taught enough to form a chord,

or melody, and slices each rainbow
curl of color, then splices, shapes
a spiral colored stair from swamp
to sky for Noah, and/or God, to descend
into all, and every mother, they drowned.

Stars & Stilettos

by Timothy Arliss OBrien

Act 1: The Galactic Poet Laureate

Scene opens with a solitary figure standing center stage in front of the stage curtain, bathed in the soft glow of starlight. The closed stage curtain is a panoramic view of a vast, glittering cosmos, with distant galaxies and swirling nebulae.

Divina Stellars *(taking a deep breath, addressing the audience)*: Welcome, my darlings, to the infinite. Out here, in the deep dark black of space, amidst the swirling galaxies and shimmering stars, is where I found my true self. And where I became, quite unexpectedly, the Galactic Poet Laureate. But let me take you back, back, back to when it all began.

Divina exits behind the curtain.

Divina Stellars *(narrating)*:
Tommy was just a kid from a small coastal town, fascinated by the ocean's mysteries and the beauty of its hidden world. Every wave that crashed on the shore whispered secrets, and every tide pulled at his little heartstrings. But Tommy had another passion, one that flowed like an undercurrent through his life.

The curtain opens and the stage is set with a single spotlight focused center stage. A chair and a small table cluttered with notebooks and marine biology textbooks rest in the spotlight. Off to the side is a clothes rack littered with sequins, feathers, and fabrics. The background is dark with subtle hints of a glittering curtain. A beautiful queen, dressed in a glamorous yet understated outfit, enters the stage and takes a deep breath. She sits on the chair, facing the audience. Her name was Tommy, and this was her story.

Divina Stellars *(reminiscing about her young self)*:

(With a youthful, tender voice)
I was just a kid, you know? A little boy with a big secret.

Growing up in a small coastal town, where boys played with balls and girls played with dolls.
But me? I played with makeup, glitter, discounted prom gowns, and with words.

(Looking down at the notebook on the table. Picks up a notebook and holds it up into the light)
This notebook became my best friend. I wrote poems about the stars, about love, about dreams, and sometimes about boys. But the one thing I felt like I couldn't write about was myself.

(Standing up, mimicking a more defensive stance)
"Why are you so different?" they'd ask. "Why don't you act like a normal boy?" They didn't understand that I was scared. Scared of their words. Scared of their fists. Scared of their rejection.

(She moves towards the audience, her voice growing stronger)
But then, one day, I found a poem. Not just any poem. A poem about beauty, strength, and about owning who you are. Those words were like magic, transforming my fear into courage. And my courage into words.

(She picks up the notebook, holding it close)
I started writing again. But this time, not just about stars and dreams and boys, but about my truth. About the boy who loved glitter and glam. About the boy who was destined to become a queen.

(Taking a deep breath, she puts down the notebook and begins to transform, shedding her plain outfit for a glamorous show stopping costume. Her voice starts embodying the strength of her drag persona)
And so, Tommy became Divina Stellars. The drag queen with a heart full of poetry and a spirit that shined brighter than any stage light.

(She mimics putting on makeup)
With every blend of blush, I wrote a new line of my story.
(She walks over to a clothes rack and throws on a boa and a feathered hat)
With every sequin and feather, I penned my triumphs and tribulations.

My poetry wasn't just on paper anymore; it was in my every move, my every performance.

(Looking out to the audience with pride)
I faced homophobia head-on, not with fists, but with verses. My words cut through hatred like a hot knife through butter or a turkey carver through hip pads. And on stage, I found not only my voice. I found myself.

My words traveled far and wide, crossing borders, transcending languages. They spoke of the ocean's plight, of the need to protect our beautiful blue planet, of the fight for LGBTQ rights. It was my mission to give a voice to the voiceless, to shine a light on the hidden corners of our world.

Drag. Drag was where I found my voice, my power. On stage, under the spotlight, I could be anything, anyone. I could be free. And it was through drag that I began to write—about love, about pain, about the beauty and fragility of our world.

And then, one day, the stars called. A message from the Galactic Federation, inviting me—me, a drag queen from Earth—to become the Galactic Poet Laureate. To travel the stars and spread my message across the cosmos.

A stagehand rushes on stage and puts a sash over Divina with writing on it saying Galactic Poet Laureate.

Divina picks up a model spaceship off the table and holds it into the light.

The Stardust, my little ship. She was as fabulous as I was. Together, we set off on a journey through the galaxy, visiting distant worlds and ancient civilizations. Each stop was a new adventure, a new audience to inspire. I traveled for 13 earth moon cycles. That's about two and half years for you novice space cadets.

She steps forward, holding a book of poems.

And these are my stories, and the transformation of all the hate and anger in the universe into love, peace, and unity.

Divina Performs a lip sync to I Am Here by P!nk with the book in her hands pressed to her chest and raised to the sky.

(She holds the book of poetry up to the light and strikes a final pose, embodying the full confidence of Divina Stellars)
I am Divina Stellars. A queen. A poet. A survivor.
And this is my story, written in stardust and sealed with a kiss.

The spotlight fades to black as Divina Stellars holds her pose, the stage shimmering with the reflection from a disco ball.

Act 2: Across the Universe

Scene opens with Divina Stellars at stage left on a vibrant alien planet wearing an outfit just as vibrant and outlandish. Exotic flora and fauna surround her as she performs for a crowd of diverse extraterrestrial beings.

Divina Stellars:
Welcome, my beautiful cosmic creatures! Today, I bring you a tale of the deep blue sea, of coral reefs and bioluminescent wonders. But it's more than just a story; it's a call to action.

She begins to recite a poem, her voice filled with passion and urgency.

Divina Stellars *(reciting)*:
On a faraway blue speck,
Where sunlight and moisture move breakneck,
Creating life of flora and fauna,
We find the setting for our first drama.

In the depths of oceans blue where sunlight fades,
Coral gardens we find brightly arrayed,
Whispers of a time now past,
Echoes of a world that is unfortunately fading fast.

We must protect these realms, so rich and so rare,
We have to guard them with an urgent tender care,
For every wave of aqua that gently rolls,
Carries the weight and the lives of countless souls.

Heed my warnings and embrace my hope
For that is the only way that life can continue to cope

The alien audience is visibly moved to cheers and applause.

(Divina Stellars steps to the front of the stage to address the audience)
And so, my message spread from planet to planet. Words that transcended species, resonating with the shared hope of a better future.

The scene transitions to stage right a high-tech conference room aboard the Stardust. Divina Stellars is turned with her back in discussion with a holographic projection of the Galactic Federation.

Galactic Federation:

Divina Stellars,

(Divina turns to the audience, points to herself)
Divina: That's me!

Galactic Federation:
Your work has united billions across the galaxy. Your poetry is a beacon of hope. But there is much more to be done. Will you help us in the fight against the devastation of some of our worlds happening in the furthermost reaches of the andromeda galaxy?

Divina Stellars: *(turning to somewhat face the audience.)*
Absolutely. Let's act now, before it's too late. Let's launch a universal initiative for environmental and sentient rights, powered by the arts and all of this gorgeous beauty.
Divina gestures towards herself.

The Counselor nods, and the hologram fades. Divina Stellars turns to face the audience.

And thus began one of my greatest challenges.
I grew up looking at the andromeda galaxy through my grandfather's telescope, imagining it was a distant glowing bioluminescent squid, or a bright sapphire rhinestone glued

right onto the nipple of the sky.
(Divina pulls away nipple pasties to reveal two big sapphires on her breasts.)

It took me three moon cycles to travel there by warpspeed. Once I got there we organized rallies, concerts, and poetry readings all across the galaxy. We harnessed the power of art to inspire change and we rallied support for the preservation of our worlds and the rights of all beings.

Divina steps to the other side of the stage to a massive rally on an alien planet. Thousands of beings from various species hold up glowing banners and signs with messages of unity and conservation.

Divina Stellars:

Clearing her throat dramatically
Greetings, intergalactic darlings! I come in peace, and with fabulous style, of course!

The aliens murmur among themselves, unsure.

Divina Stellars:

Striking a pose
Now, I know you're wondering—who is this radiant creature before us?
Well, I am Divina Stellars, a drag queen and The Galactic Poet Laureate,

A stagehand rushes onto stage and puts the poet laureate sash on Divina.

And I am here to sprinkle some glitter on your galaxy and speak beautiful words of affirmation and hope!
For the time of division and aggression has come to an end and the time of unity and love is upon us!

The aliens exchange confused glances.

Divina Stellars:

Holds up her hand, palm out
Let's talk about something truly universal: love, acceptance, and the right to to be beautiful, regardless of what planet you hail from!

One alien, a bright green blob, raises a tentacle.

Divina Stellars:
Yes little tentacled alien blob, do you have a question?

Alien Blob:
With a quizzical gurgle
Can we all be beautiful? Can we all be loved?

Divina Stellars: *(Hearty Laugh)*
Oh, honey darling beautiful blob creature,
Beauty is that twinkle in your eye, that sass in your step, the confidence that makes you feel like you could conquer the universe! And we can all achieve that by extending love to one another. No matter how different your tentacles or fur are from one another.

Alien Blob:
With a quizzical gurgle
These aren't tentacles, this is a hat.

Divina Stellars:

Well, regardless That is a cute hat, I am going to have to get the hologram number for your haberdashery.

Look to the skies beautiful alien creatures
All sentient beings have been experiencing this disunity and uprising division.
But let me tell you a secret.

Leans in, stage whisper
We all shine brighter together.
Especially when we all love one another
And can see the beauty in every living creature.

She straightens, launching into a poetic monologue.

Divina Stellars:

In the vastness of the stars,
Every being, near and far,
Deserves to love, to laugh, to play,
In their own unique, queer way.

From galaxies to tiny moons,
We all can dance to our own tunes.
Different colors, shapes, and forms,
Embrace the love that truly warms.

So whether you're a blob or star,
A dazzling queen or a creature seeming so bizarre,
Remember this, oh cosmic friends,
Unity is where hatred ends.

The aliens begin to nod, some clapping their tentacles together in appreciation.

Divina Stellars:

Bowing with flair
Let's turn this galaxy into a runway of love and acceptance!
Who's with me?

The aliens cheer, lifting their appendages high.

Divina Stellars:
Laughing joyously
That's the spirit! Now, who's ready to dance and work this runway like no asteroid is watching?

Music starts playing, and Divina Stellars operforms for the aliens a fabulous lip sync to Weapons by Ava Max, twirling and laughing, bridging worlds with style and grace.

Divina Stellars:
Steps forward to address the audience.

From the depths of the oceans to the furthest reaches of space, I fought, with beauty and love. And slowly, change began to take root. Governments listened, local agencies and commissions were held accountable, and communities came together like never before.

Third Act: "The Galactic Peace Mission"

Scene opens with Divina Stellars, the Galactic Poet Laureate, standing on her ship as before in front of a hologram of the Galactic Federation.

Galactic Federation:
(With a serious tone)
Divina Stellars, we need your help. A division rages at the edge of the Milky Way against the Andromeda galaxy. To bring unity, you must retrieve the Flute of Peace and the Glockenspiel of Love from a desolate, dreary planet.

Divina Stellars:
(Flipping her hair dramatically)
Darling, you had me at "Glockenspiel."
What's life without a little adventure and a fabulous little musical accessory?

The council nods, somewhat confused but optimistic

Council Leader:
(With a serious tone)
But be warned Divina,
This planet is dark, isolated, and dreary. Anyone that travels there falls into an emotional spiral and is overcome with their deepest darkest depressions.

Divina Stellars:
You know, depression tried to take me down once, but I said, 'Honey, you picked the wrong queen! I'm too funny and fabulous to flop and frown!'

Council Leader:
Safe travels beautiful poet, and may all the love and peace you have spread during your reign be with you now more than ever.

Divina Exits the Stage

Scene shifts to the desolate planet. The landscape is gray and gloomy, a stark contrast to Divina Stellars's vibrant outfit. She steps cautiously, the weight of the planet's oppressive aura visible.

Divina Stellars:
You know, darlings, when the Galactic Federation mentioned a "desolate" planet, I thought, "How bad could it be?" But this place? It's like a bar with no drag show: no sequins or glitter in sight! This planet needs a new coat of makeup and some bigger lashes!

Pauses, taking a deep breath.

Truth is, I'm scared. This planet pulls you into a pit of gloom, like the time I wore a beige outfit to brunch—no sparkle, no life.
It reminds me of my past, those days when I thought the world was too dark to handle a queen like me.

I'm desperately trying to remember why I do this. If I can bring a little light, a little love, even here, then maybe, just maybe, we can turn this planet into a runway for all things beautiful.

So, I'll face my fears, armed with my stilettos and sass, because nothing can dull the shine of a true queen! Now these magical musical instruments must be around here somewhere.

Divina ventures further onto stage looking for the magical artiface.
Holding her arms out, theatrically

Divina Stellars:
Honestly, this place makes my ex's apartment look like a tropical paradise!

This place could use a serious makeover. I'm thinking disco balls and neon lights!

As she explores, she experiences flashbacks of her childhood, hearing echoes of homophobic remarks.

Voiceover:
Echoing cruel words "Why are you so different? You don't

belong!"
"You'll never be a real man!" "You're a weak sissy!" "Why can't you just be normal?"

Divina Stellars:
Pausing, taking a deep breath
Oh no, the pain and anguish from my childhood feels all too near once again.

More voices echo around her mimicking all the hate and ugly words that were spoken to her as a child growing up.

Divina Stellars:
I'm not quite feeling like myself anymore.

The lights around her flash as she transforms into a monochrome outfit, shedding the color she had been wearing.

shadows start dancing around her

Divina Stellars:
Oh no! My color! I don't know if I can go on!
If only I could remember joy, like the time my last boyfriend took me to zoo and we got fresh behind the ornithology house. Or the time that fashion atelier house reached out to me to custom design a gown as matte black as the sky with thousands of starlike rhinestones.

Divina Pauses

Or the time I was awarded a grant from the Oregon Arts Commision and performed new genre breaking music at The Clinton Street Theater, at First Christian Church in Eugene, and at the New Music Gathering at Lincoln Hall.

The shadows around her dissipate, the murmuring voices fade away, and at the corner of the stage in a small cave there is a small treasure chest that starts to shimmer and glow.

Divina Stellars:
My memories! The joy I hold in my chest from days past is breaking the curse!
And Look! There is something shining and beautiful! Is it a

rhinestone gown? Lasers and lights from a disco ball?
Divina rushes to the chest:
Oh, it's just an old treasure chest.
Maybe it has some new wigs in it!

She opens the chest and pulls out the Flute of Peace and the Glockenspiel of Love

Divina Stellars: *holding the instruments into the light*
Who knew peace and love were hidden away in such a dark desolate place?
We need to get this out into the world and share their beautiful sounds with everyone!

Divina plays a melody on the flute of peace and color starts to come to the stage.
Then she plays a few notes on the glockenspiel and the stage bursts forth in color and music.
Divina transforms into a vibrantly colored dress and hair.

Divina Stellars:
I broke the curse! I must call the Galactic Federation and tell them. But first we have to celebrate!

Divina begins to lip sync to Let There Be Love by Christian Aguilera to celebrate breaking the curse.

Divina Stellars:
There's always time for a celebratory lip sync,
Now lots go spread this peace and love!

Divina rushes off the stage.

Scene transitions to the conflict of andromeda against the milky way. Divina Stellars stands between the two alien armies, both sides poised for battle.

Divina Stellars:
I am Divina Stellars, Named The Galactic Poet Laureate by the Galactic Federation.
Stage hand rushes on stage and puts the poet laureate sash on Divina.
Listen to my words, and take in the music of peace and unity.

The crowds grow quiet, and the lights focus on Divina.

She raises the Flute of Peace to her lips, playing a soothing melody.

Divina Stellars:
In the vastness of the sky,
We all have a reason to fly.
Different colors, shapes, and dreams,
Together we are brighter than all these divisive schemes.

Set aside the fear and hate,
It is love that makes us great.
Embrace each soul, unique and rare,
And create a universe that thrives for all with care.

Hand in hand, let's stand as one,
As an age of unity has begun.
Celebrate what makes us free,
In unity we will find our peace and harmony.

Divina plays from the glockenspiel of love

The Galactic Federation projects as a hologram onto the back of the stage

The Galactic Federation:
You did it Divina!
You did it!
You brought peace and unity to the galaxy with your words and with your music!

Divina Stellars:
Oh, honey, you'd be surprised what a little music and love can do!
Winking, then playing the Glockenspiel of Love, adding a playful rhythm

Listen up, cosmic cuties! We're all stardust, floating in this vast universe.
Is this really how we want to spend our precious time?
Fighting when we could be dancing?

The aliens and the federation cheer.

We've all got our battles, but the real strength lies in unity and acceptance.
Let's trade in our hate and judgment for some fabulous bling, and a dance party where all are welcome!

Galactic Federation:
Yeah, we love a dance party!

Divina Stellars:

Triumphant, addressing the crowd
Remember, love conquers all! Now, who's ready for a cosmic dance party?

Divina plays the glockenspiel again, and the music spreads into a joyful celebration, with Divina celebrating with a joyful lip sync to Magic by Kylie Minogue.

The scene ends with Divina Stellars in the center, the galaxies united in peace, as she looks up at the stars.

Divina Stellars:
With a wink
Another day, another galaxy was saved. Now, where's my next adventure?

Curtain falls as the stage glimmers with newfound hope and unity.

Finale: a postlogue

Divina Stellars comes out in front of the curtain, looking up at the stars in a beautiful evening gown, mounds of expensive jewelry, and her poet laureate sash.

Divina Stellars:
My journey through the stars has taught me that we are all connected. Every life, every world, is a thread in the vast tapestry of the universe. And it is our duty to protect and cherish each and every one.

She begins to recite another poem, her voice soft but filled with determination.

Divina Stellars *(reciting)*:
From stardust we are born anew,
A cosmic dance in endless blue,
Together, we must find our way,
To brighter nights and clearer days.

And as the Galactic Poet Laureate,
Divina is already wearing her poet laureate sash but a stagehand rushes out anyway
Divina waves him back off stage
I promise I will continue to use my voice, and my art, to inspire and to fight for what is right. For the oceans of Earth, for the beauty of our universe, and for the rights of every living being.

So, my darlings, as you go forth into your own lives, remember this:
Your voice matters. Your actions matter. And your words matter.
Together, we can create a future where love, beauty, and justice reign supreme.
From the depths of the oceans to the furthest stars, we are all connected.
And we are all responsible for the world we leave behind.

The spotlight fades, leaving only the glow of the stars.

Divina Stellars *(voiceover)*:
Thank you, my beautiful stars, for sharing this journey with me.
Let's make our universe a masterpiece.

End of play.

Smoking Chief

by Lindsay Baik

The Unicorns
by Sarah Das Gupta

In the half-light I saw them first:
galloping through strands of grey mist
which drifted wraith-like across the fields,
their hooves leaving light imprints
on the cushioned grass.

Their chiselled white heads, disembodied
floated past in the growing gloom
as if propelled by some strange force.
Their white manes mingled with the mist,
like drifts of snow floating on the wind.

Their white tails blew out behind them,
framed, outlined by the surrounding darkness.
Single silver horns, banded by circles of gold
impaled the drifting wisps of mist
with proud assurance.

They galloped towards the dark fringe of the forest
under the brooding, threatening pine trees.
The sound of a hundred hooves now silenced
by the green carpets of the winter pine needles,
a ghostly herd.

Waiting beneath a stand of great oaks,
the pale Queen of the Northern ice fields
held aloft a golden bowl exquisitely engraved
with polar bears, walrus, seals and Arctic wolves,
an object of impossible beauty.

The unicorns encircled her,
knees bent in dutiful obeisance.
Above in the bare, stark boughs,
white birds perched
like great powder puffs.
A horn began to sound.

In the Dim Coming Times
by Marianne Taylor

After W. B. Yeats

In the dim coming times, vaccines won't hold
against the waves of milky greenish foam
bourne by ill birds, cattle and swine,
and some will succumb to the mutating thing.
Flesh will rot and fall away, soulless
eyes burn hollow and gray, spoiled milk where once
fish swam. Gnawing hunger will raise these up,
shabby, disheveled and slow, this plague will advance.

Though we'll prime our Bushmasters, hone our knives,
stock underground pantries with ammo and cans,
these vagrant hordes will smell our stunned silence,
their shrill hunger sound, and en masse stagger
upon us to feast on that which keeps us free.
Then Eastward, ravenous, we'll all shamble on.

Tokyo
by Brian Park

Pulled In
by Grace Lee

Maroon red, lilac purple, amber gold.
Aurora colors on the swooping wings
Of fragile butterflies. It jumps from leaf
To leaf and flashes its grand wings to watchers.
A beautiful bright view, the watchers say.

If only their eyes shifted to the side:
A moth with dull greyed wings sits on a wall.
It is the dark sky—twinkling stars surround it.
It is the canvas on which butterflies shine.

Its eyes spot flickering red flames on candles
With shining vivid shades like sunset glow.
Dull wings take flight, petite feet land on the
Melting wax stand. It tiptoes closer, then
Too close.

Flame touches, then spreads, then envelopes it.
Fire eats its wings, thus forming deadly sheens.
Fire steals its limbs in a colossal blur.
Remains then sprinkle down as smoky ash.
A startling bright view as it fully burns.

Now, I approach the dark tight alley that
May be my flame. My mind is on fire, and
My daring burns away. But people flutter
Around me, mingling, giggling, and make me
A shadow like dull gray smoked ashes, yet
I am pulled in.

MINUTES FROM THE LOCAL AREA NETWORK PARTY

by RJ Equality Ingram

3
Children mine under the desert for their food
Boarders expand far past their short noses
As they chip at the walls w/ stone pickaxes
Always one jump scare away from oblivion
Their leader wafts attention away from wrath
By sacrificing his own holdings he vanishes
Now the team can get back to the real work
Excavating through torn up abandoned mines
But first let me tell you about how we got here
Once there was a well & inside a lost squid
The villagers didn't know what they were doing
They fed on scraps & prayed in the corners
And then my son who is not a hero freed them
From the supposed hauntings of their wildness

2
At home my son awakens fresh & evenly wild
Static robbed him of his rank & possessions
So much can be said about rebirth that isn't
He scrambles together an inventory shoddy
Yet necessary as it's a day's walk to the desert
He does not eat he is not hungry resurgence
Doesn't cost the stomach anything anymore
His name is his only armor now & yes I envy
Anyone's ability to walk right out of the house
Having just lost a great battle & greater still
Night as it envelops him like a quiet snowfall
It is late when he arrives back on the scene
And before he can rejoin the group his body
Greets another quick death from an arrow

1
Mortality hangs for some like a brass knocker
Atop a threshold of an endless chrome palace
Each rap comes w/ a tiny cost that adds up

And the cards get reshuffled into new patters
For others like myself we just keep on running
Around the place until we tire ourselves into
Submission or another fancier word for peace
Exhausting options feels like the only choice
When my sone wakes again from his last death
He is mad & embarrassed & still only human
I must confess I cannot assist his wandering
So I watch him stumble around making fresh
Mistakes as each wonderful blunder awakens
An invigorating drive into his wounded heart

0
Regrettably I lied to my son after his first death
We had no idea more were to follow so I said
Not again you must never leave w/out us again
How was I to know he would take up fleeting
As a profession? Kids today keep dangerous
Hobbies & the best boundaries we could draw
Were those around overindulgences & war
Resurgence is a weapon that can't be weirded
And now we wait for the one great rebellion
That might eradicate allegiances to the divine
Drive that keeps him from staying in the grave
And brings him back to us even harder still
From adolescence grows the desire for more
How dangerous the unquenchable do become

Bonus Life
And if you asked him he would say it is normal
For a kid & friends to wander into the unknown
Passages w/ nothing but wit & an empty sack
We are all clear they say back to each other
When a new cavern opens onto untold nothing
That's when you asked the coin to fall face up
Just one more time please just one more time
And when it does wonder to who exactly do you owe
This extra life to but no one can answer back
We are all clear they said in the white room
While you held onto threads pulling through
To another chance victory bc every last life
Is a bonus life & you see that in his scarred eyes
The way the blue earths turn again & again

Season of Fall

by Ryan Kim

Sometimes
by Marianne Taylor

your eyes are closed but
you still feel the light and you

wonder what will bite from
within the dark portals. water

flows through the portals and
you ride it in into the beyond

which is rough and choppy but
thrilling and splashy too. you see

the other shore so you climb
and you feel that you're thinking

but the clock says it's time to build
a house on mossy ground where

birds are smokey and flowers all red
and singeing fires flagrantly burn

this is not hell although you can
smell sulphur there are other more

fragrant smells and you think but
you musn't so you feel the sound

of a door that is cold and steely and
you see chicken wire pressed be-

tween panes of glass in this place
you are confined you are captive

now and you know you've been tor-
tured. violet petals cover your limp

body and everything's fine.

Red Dragon Eros
by James Hall

The red dragon climbs,
wings unfurled,
flapping, snapping, taut
like sails catching a sudden squall,
soaring toward the sun.

The raptor, breath scorching,
screeches her mating call.
Molting, armor shredded,
purging, new skin glistening
each year at Lupercalia.

Dragon scales, forged of fire,
pointed red hearts,
languidly falling, dillydally
drifting through wispy cirrus clouds
souls searching for a home.

Ardor dissipated, a disheveled
Old Bard's battered lute
beseeches coin from lovers,
at the feast of Lupercal.
Showers of hearts fall from on high.

As Bard's grasping hand is pierced
by barbed heart, great warmth flows,
longing rekindles love within.
No one is immune to desire,
born of Red Dragon's Eros fire.

Untitled
by Yoon Park

The Visitor

by Anna Classon

Bella always thought that vampires were supposed to be sexy, at least that was how all of her books described them. The pale man in dark clothes and a cape currently raiding her kitchen was decidedly not sexy at all. Bella had originally come downstairs for a glass of water, but was met with something much more interesting. As if the being smelled her standing there, he turned around.

"Who are you?" crumbs flew out of his mouth and littered the floor. He seemed just as surprised to see her standing there as she was to see him.

"I'm Bella. I kind of live here," she said slowly, trying to play down her fear. "Who are you?"

"My name is Blade." The being licked his fingers and continued rummaging around.

"What a nice, normal, and totally reassuring name," Bella murmured. "What are you doing in my house?"

"I'm just scavenging food. Do you have any idea how hard it is to feed yourself when you're allergic to the sun?" He ripped the pantry door off its hinges and started to tear through it, shelf by shelf.

"Well you should really work on your execution. You woke me up with all the noise," said Bella, who was growing more annoyed than fearful now. "My parents are going to be down here any second, so I suggest you get out of here."

"No they aren't, I made sure of that."

"What?"

"Oh, I didn't kill them, heavens no. Sleep dust, very effective. I guess I missed your room, damn munchies got the best of me." The being continued to tear through Bella's kitchen, unbothered by her presence.

"Don't vampires usually drink blood anyway?"

He turned around this time and smiled, which revealed a set of terrifyingly sharp fangs. "Yeah, I'm just tired of it lately. Honestly, I was craving more of a sweet treat."

Bella blinked. "The door to your left is the freezer, have at it."

"Yes, chipwiches!"

"So is this whole 'breaking into someone's house, destroying it, and then eating all their food' thing a regular routine?"

"Kind of. We aren't exactly a huge population, so it's not hard. When something like this happens though, that's when we have to make a decision," Blade sat down, leaning against the only intact cabinet in the kitchen and looked at Bella. "Some of us will actually consider killing humans as an option, but I won't do it. I was human once too and I remember how scary it was to transform. So, I always go the sleep dust route. It's non-violent, and only erases the parts of your memory that involve me."

"How generous," said Bella.

"Well, my other options are to turn you into a vampire and make you disappear leaving your parents in an endless state of worry, or to kill you. So pick your poison."

"What if I swore to keep your secret."

"People lie."

"Okay, well what if I said that if I tell anyone, you can come back and kill me?"

Blade considered this.

"Deal." Blade moved towards the door. Before he left, he grabbed Bella's hand.

She hissed and pulled her hand back. "What the hell?" A small circular mark had appeared on her palm.

"If you break the promise, this little spot will kill you. It's called a marker, and we can choose to activate it. It'll be a quick death, but I don't recommend it. Consider it an insurance policy."

"Okay. Feel free to get out of my house now," said Bella fearfully. Blade flashed his teeth at her in a sly smile, whipped his cape over his face, and disappeared. Bella stared at the empty water glass in her hand for a long time before crossing through the carnage in her kitchen to fill it.

The Webb Telescope
by Lynette G. Esposito

discovered
stars were buttons.
If a human could reach them,
the world would change.

The sky remains bright
with eyes
that blink a known reality of beauty
untouched by man
who in his ignorance, is filled
with a wild passion
to change everything.

Maze

by Jahin Claire Oh

Fantasia
by Aletha Irby

for Mallarmé

From the grand fountain
Of fonts and gilded calligraphies
Uncial and Old English
Italic and the irrepressibly
Fecund Batarde
Frolics forth the letter ***F***
My favorite scriven as a schoolgirl
For it was foliate with serifs as a forest
Fraught as wrought iron
As the fauna and flora
Who flock to and flummox
The four-letter faultline
Resonant as well with forenoon's
Flautist of a faun
Composing a lullaby for his newborn
Among the bluebelled woodlands of ambient Albion
An infant who will grow
To freckled and feckless adolescence
Farouche as fornication
Fickle as Fortuna or pianoforte
All foghorn and fippleflute
Unfettered and fascinated by the unprincely frog's
Amphibian tongue resplendent
With a dragonfly dinner *al fresco*
By Chef Fitzhugh "Phoenix" Terwilliger
His newest culinary creation
Polliwogs and Firebirds Au Fromage
Near the frond-swollen pond
An art as unforesworn and unforeseen
As the diaries of the demimonde
A force to be reckoned with.

COMMUNICATION WITH THE OTHER

by John Grey

Our sun was dying.
Most of us stayed behind
to slowly die with it.
But a few booked passage
on space ships,
with no particular destination,
no plan in mind,
other to extend our lives
in relative comfort,
for as long as our fuel lasted.

That we have landed here
is sheer happenstance.
We are not tourists.
We are not an invading force.
We are merely desperate.
It's most likely we can't
breathe your air
or eat your food.
And our rockets
were damaged on impact.
So we cannot move on from here.

Please let us
hunker down in our cocoons,
live out the rest of our existence
in dignity.
Forget any great knowledge-swap
You have little to learn from us
because we have nothing much to tell.

It's comfortable here
in this garden
shaded by your –
what do you call them – roses.
A red sky just like the one back home.
But, thank god, for different reasons.

Untitled

by Yoon Park

To Walk Away From Wonder
by Nicholas Yandell

"You're living in a fantasy". My whole life that's what they've told me.

"You're just that *head in the clouds* type, who inhales dreams, like they're something of substance.

Who laughs to oneself and laughs out loud. Whose reckless eyes are stigmatized, as an unstable amalgamation of restless energy and immersive introspection."

They say: "Aimless wanderer, who do you pretend you are? Go dip your starry eyes, into your wishing well, and hoist yourself out, sobered and straightened. It's time to walk away from the push and pull of the untethered void. Draw some thick hard lines between the real world and illusions. The tangible and the *not worthwhile*. The useful and useless."

But I've never been able to ignore that realm of mystery, just because it's misunderstood by those around me. The whispers in the air, beyond the crackling state of stirred-up sensations. The pounding pulse of vitality, beyond any physicality, in the realm of possibility.

So that's why I'm out here, trudging through dream marshes, a pen as my walking stick, a notebook as my map. Sketching out my odyssey, to the far-flung borders of the imaginary, illustrating these unconscious epics as images of the awakened state.

This is just one of many treks, released from the known and inhabiting the disconnect. I'm still here, grounded on familiar earth, but diverging into multiple realms. Operating interdimensionally, never severed. Existing simultaneously, crossing occasionally, melding often, but sometimes, contrastingly jarring in juxtaposition.

Through specks of creation, pulled from flows of speculation, gushing from the salvaged chunks of dreamscapes I was never supposed to retain. I'm perpetually lured by these cherished relics of shadow existence, which far too often come bobbing to the surface, at the most inopportune instances. Amidst the traffic flow of the present, I'm left glitching with drifting desires, jamming the steady projections and interrupting the static screens.

There's a painful pull from disparate worlds, leaving so little chance to settle. A state of adaptive discomfort I yearn to subside. Because I've tried all other potential remedies to curb the cravings and satisfy my needs. I'd read the surgeon general's warnings against meddling with the mechanisms of the unconscious. I've seen those harbingers of neon danger, detailing a slow poisoning of the memory bank, with each undisturbed illusion. I've noted all the side effects of seeking my destinations and I'm not turning back.

The aches are just symptoms of transition. Stretching pains that will soon fade into normalcy, once my mind finally gains flexibility. And with a twinge of lucidity, I'll finally say: I was always meant to straddle numerous worlds. I'm just not quite there yet, but I'm on my way.

So yes. It's true. I have been living in a fantasy, when I've been fortunate enough to have the opportunity, and I won't hide it anymore. I'm making peace with my illusions and accepting them as part of my whole. And I can handle the vaporous breathing, as long as I can still drift freely. Happily embracing the unknown, but with just one little piece of surety. I can now see myself with much more clarity, so on the rest of this long journey, whether pushed away or pulled asunder, I'll know that I was never meant to walk away from wonder.

Roots of Life
by Ryan Kim

The Girl Who Fed On Nightmares
by Aeesha Abdullahi Alhaji

i saw an owl
cried twice before
dawn
with the night as an alibi
i see mortals in mourning clothes
my mother sets
her dreamcatcher,
she collects all my nightmares
in one
basket & eats them overnight.
i see my brother in the moon orbs
he lives on through cycle of rebirths
i carry his soul in my mouth,
a reincarnated cherry from a random pick of autumn
a dead end to the matyrs who lived till
through dying breaths,
re-writing fate with
a pen made from branches
of a tree that weighs our sins.

Close Encounter of the Black-Death Kind

by Tom Holmes

from a report dated Thursday, March 20, 1355 (after Vespers)

And then one astrologer
one past night discovered a star
birth another star that grew
to part the clouds, spin, and drop
beyond the village swamp:

"I found nothing there
with smoke plumeing out
of nothing above me. Something
barbaric bleated or shrieked
as I whimpered my rite prayers.

They shone silver and green,
tall as me, with giant opal eyes.
They touched me. It felt like god
abandoning me before harming me
once again for the final, last time.

They were clean. With intent,
they pissed in the lake, the river.
The well twinkled like gold
that turns to lead. They touched rats'
fleas. God, everything was poison.

They departed within a wink
and smile. This was before
my children only bore twenty-two
adult teeth, they too having
been touched, as if by God."

Bearded Man--

by Lindsay Baik

The Return of Excalibur

by Sarah Das Gupta

The last of King Arthur's knights
took the sword Excalibur by the hilt
and hurled it back into the lake.
The Sword formed an elegant arc
as it flew through the midnight sky.
Its jewelled hilt flashed in the light
of the ghostly, pale winter moon.
Rubies, diamonds, emeralds, pearls
shone and glittered, challenging the stars
which so brightly paved the Milky Way.

From the depths of the lake,
a hand arose, mystic, wonderful,
draped in the whitest damask.
It seized the shimmering hilt,
and waved it thrice above the water,
slicing and cutting through the frosty air.
Slowly, Excalibur vanished
beneath the black and secret waters.

A dark boat floated smoothly
across the silent lake.
Inside sat three veiled queens,
to take the wounded King
to rest and recover at Avalon.
To return in England's hour of need,
to sleep and wait,
the once and future King.

Final Liquidation— Everything Must Go

by Philip Athans

"Kinda beautiful in its own way, isn't it?" a voice behind me said.

I nodded, still looking up into the indigo sky. A whirlpool of purple and blue light, throwing off sparks of white, filled the dome of stars. Rising up into its center from the soaring peak that dominated the western horizon was a kilometers-wide column of black-brown… What did they call it?

"Ejecta?" the voice asked, startling me. I turned around, almost tripped on one of the sample cases, and when I realized I must have been speaking aloud—at least that last part—I smiled as quickly and as sincerely as I could.

"Ejecta… from the volcano," the little tellian woman said, still smiling. Her skin was a deep forest green with a subtle brown mottling. The single eye scanning me was at once sparkling and dull.

Still smiling, I said, "Ejecta, yes. From the volcano."

"Kinda beautiful in its own way, isn't it?" she said again, pointing briefly up into the silent disturbance in the sky.

I nodded but didn't look back. "It is," I said, and it was—a beautiful whirlpool of charged particles and burning ejecta and the shimmering remnants of the little planet's atmosphere being drained away into…?

"Hell if I know," the woman said, shrugging—and I know I hadn't spoken that time.

Crap, I thought, and watched her react to it.

"A whole cargo container, eh?" she asked.

I nodded.

"All toys?" she asked.

I nodded again and clicked open the sample case on the folding table in front of her. A child laughed somewhere in the market and as I closed my mind off to the little tellian, I hoped it would help. I spun the case around and she blinked twice at me, which gave me the feeling she'd felt my mind close to her. She had to know I wouldn't have made it a year in this business if any random tellian or psikey knew what I was thinking instead of hearing what I was saying. I was a little disappointed in myself that she'd read as much of me as she had—must be the distraction of the wormhole slowly sucking the planet dry.

"How many of each?" she asked, looking down her stubby nose at my product.

"I can let you have the whole container," I said, still smiling. Sales 101: Make it sound like you're doing them a favor by "allowing" them to buy more of your stuff.

The tellian shrugged and said, "I like the little… What are those little guys? The little animal kinda guys?"

"Teddy bears," I said, reaching down to take the little teddy bear out of the sample case to hand it to her.

She took it in her top left hand and squeezed it a little. "Teddy bear… What does that mean?"

I shrugged and said, "No idea. But kids love them."

She reached out to hand me the teddy bear back but I wasn't going to take it from her.

Also Sales 101.

"You'll own the teddy bear market on Ranna, Miss…?" I said.

"Flo," she said, "and leave off the miss."

"Of course. So what do you think? I can give you a price—

and I mean a price."

"Can't do it," she said, trying to hand the teddy bear back to me again. "Mister…?"

"Depner," I said, "Jim Depner—call me Jimmy. And I know you can, Flo."

Flo shook her head and replied, "Not as long as this keeps up, Jimmy."

"Sorry?"

She tipped her chin up to the sky behind me and I didn't bother turning around. I could feel the disaster in the sky behind me.

"Sure, sure," I said—how could I pretend this wasn't happening? "But you heard that kid laugh just now. I know you did." I pointed with my thumb at the almost deserted market square behind me. This was the forty-third largest city on Ranna—out of forty-nine cities—but even then, the place was a goddamn graveyard. "There are still kids, even in these unprecedented times. And now more than ever they could use the distraction of… What have we got here?"

I started rummaging around in the sample case "at random," picking up… "This is a puzzle. You slide the tiles around and it makes the picture of… some… other kind of animal. This one is like playing ping-pong by yourself—with the ball attached to the paddle by a thin elastic—"

"The hell is ping-pong?" she asked.

I just kept going. "Fill this up with water then you push these little buttons and try to get the little balls to fall into these little nets here… See that? Look at all the colors."

"Look," she said, crossing her bottom arms over her distended abdomen, "when everything goes back to normal, I'll take a bunch of the teddy bears at least, but with everything going on—"

"I heard it's closing already," I said. It was a lie, and obvious enough that she didn't need telepathy to spot it. "Okay, sorry, y'know, but, people are saying it's not… that wormholes like that eventually just burn out, or whatever. Don't you want to be prepared, nicely stocked up, when it does?"

She shook her head but said, " The whole container, eh? How many of each of these things?"

"It's, like, a thousand cases."

"Of each toy?"

I shook my head, smiled all the wider, and spread my hands out over the gray plastic case, somewhere between a briefcase and suitcase, and said, "Sample cases. You get a thousand or so sample cases."

"I'm not in the wholesale business," she said, shaking her head. She took half a step back away from the table—a huge red flag.

"No, no, no, I know," I covered, not letting my smile falter for a moment. "That's the thing… Neither is Toyarama Toyco. Anymore."

I tipped my head to the right, hands out to my sides, grinning.

"I have no idea what you mean."

I sighed. Sometimes—almost never, but sometimes—a sigh can close somebody. "The company that makes these is gone, Flo. Out of business. Dried up, closed up, moved out, liquidated. You get the last of their line—sample cases for sales people they never even hired. You can sell them as is—a fun case o' toys—or break them up and move the individual items. Or both. Whatever you want to do."

She took that half step closer again, and looked down at the teddy bear in her hand. Then her eye drifted around the nearly empty market. "Yeah… that might be a swell thing, I guess, all things being equal. I mean, once everything goes back to normal."

She looked back up at the sky behind me and her face sagged a little. She squeezed the teddy bear.

I couldn't help it. I turned and looked back up at the wormhole and the ejecta column. The breeze from behind me tickled the back of my neck. The wind on Ranna always blew in one direction now: up the slopes of the massive super-volcano and out into space and into the infinite wherever.

"So look," I said, my back still to her. "I gotta get rid of these things." I turned back to face her and she looked at me and I said, "Name your price."

"Sorry, Jimmy, I just—"

The ground started to quiver and we both stood there looking down at our feet, holding our breath for about thirty seconds, then it passed.

"If I don't sell these here, I can't get my ship out of quarantine," I said.

Sales 201: If all else fails, tell the truth.

She seemed sad, if her eye visibly shrinking in the middle of her face meant "sad," and said, "Well, the colonial authority won't let ships on- or off-planet while this is going on anyway."

My face registered "sad" in the traditional human way.

She held the teddy bear out to me again and I shook my head, closed the case, and said, "Keep it. For your kids."

"Don't have any," she replied, "but thanks."

I turned to leave, not bothering to take the second case on the dusty ground at my feet either. "Thanks for your time."

"Hey," she said as I walked away, "seriously, though, try me again when everything opens back up."

Untitled
by Yoon Park

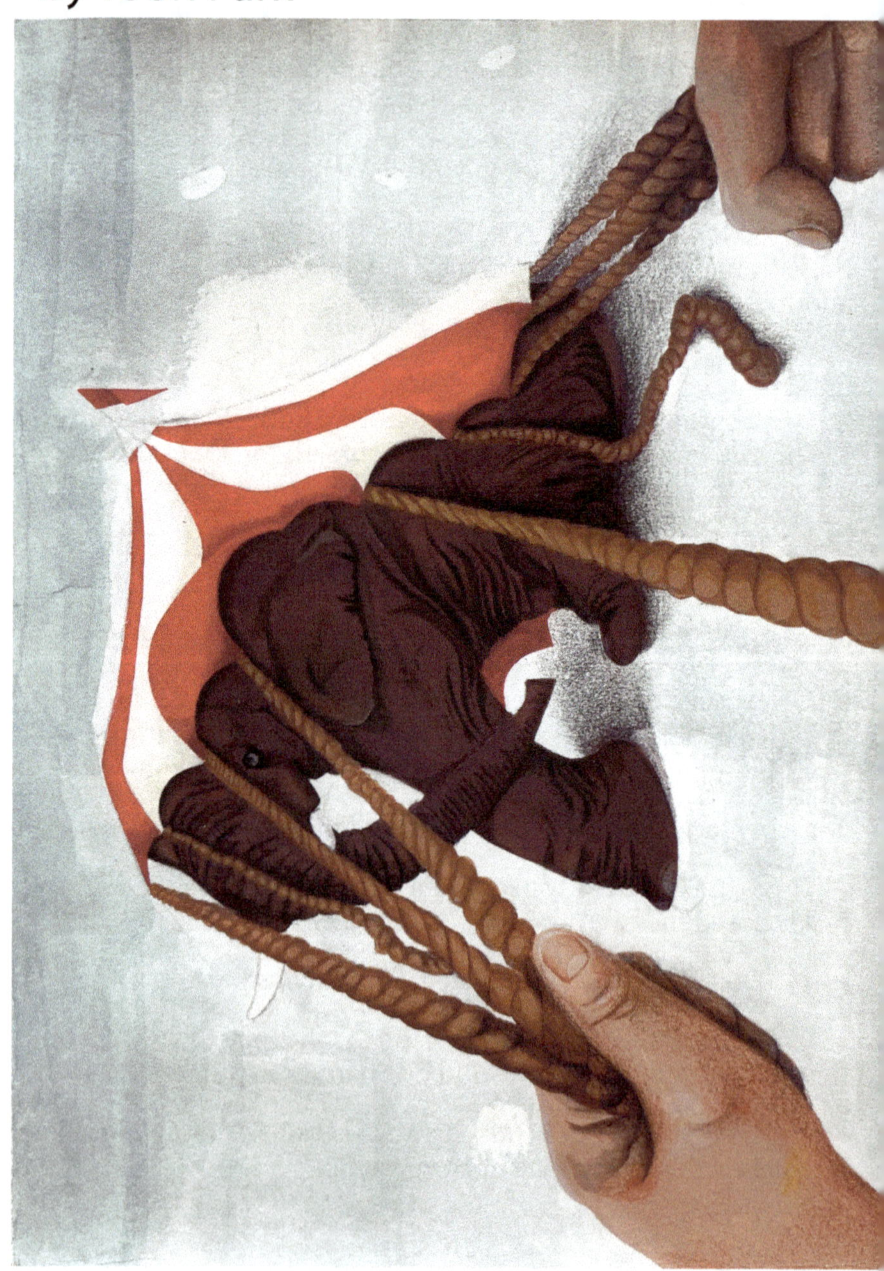

A BOTANIST ON ZANZIBUL
by John Grey

Rank towers of rholoub look drained,
snap to the touch, a cigarette-stain yellow;
but, like lambs that love their own slaughter,
fat threbolds are sucked in by the saucy, heady blooms.

On steamy afternoons, I find those threbolds
half-comatose but still sucking on petal blur,
passionately sipping the violet blood,
feet stuck in place, copper eyes unguent-dulled.

Overnight, the wide chunky petals drip with threbolds.
Come morning, it's the plant's turn to feed,
nibble like a spider on its trapped intruders.
To me, the odor of rholoub feasting is raw and caustic,

prompts an agitation in each nostril,
a queasiness in the stomach.
To threbolds this is a blessed place to die,
better than the stinging execution of the hive.

All night, they cling like fruit on a tree
so their host can rejuvenate with pleasure.

Heart of Elena

by Marianne Taylor

Once upon a mountaintop
above the cloudy seas
with burning jewels, wind-woven chants
and scent of sun-glad trees
a child discerned her destiny.

And so she descended the granite slopes
to a cottage small and remote
where humble parents with bent, gray heads
clad her in linen and wool
taught her to garden and watched her grow.

A prince's love lured her away
in a chariot rusty but just
to a colder place outside the gates
where they labored in shadowy mills
till she and her children fell blue and ill.

Evenings the demons came
to taunt and offer escape she took
their cups brought sleep and shrieking dreams
that blackened and broke the shell
of her heart. The prince could only weep.

But he planted a seed that eventually flamed
fanned by a far-off breeze and
memories of music re-grew by notes
and colored her fingers free
to weave a mat of magic reeds

to carry her people above the dark
and icy pools of woe and up
the vertical walls and back
to citrus air and jeweled rays
plumed goddesses and song.

You'll say, "So what?" and well you may

there's nothing here that's new.
And yet this slip of silk will help
begin a braid to win again the
feathered thing that flew.

Find Me In Your Memory

by Aeesha Abdullahi Alhaji

upstairs in my memory
lives a room so dark
it absorbs the planet
looking like there's no
soul behind them,
a shadow puddle of
nothingness
stands unscrambled.
floating around like air
firstly glory appears &
doom
comes after solstice
& my soul never grows
nice aftermath winters
but i feel the loss of
cherry blossoms
so find me in time
& existence
embracing the flowers
that dreamt of
the moon swallowing
my
night & dreams.

THE DREAM OF RUBY RHOD
by RJ Equality Ingram

I held up a man stronger than myself & carried both of us to a
strange river forked in a hidden forest / he called out my name
while looking past my face & into the black satin sky that
stretched from behind the trees / neither of us hailed from that
sapphire moon we learned to call home / I'll never know if he
was looking for a particular star to cry out to or if it was my face
he refused to see / before us were plants undiscovered until
after our redressing our boots & suits crunched & covered their
lavender shoots & reeds / Ruby was my mother's name until I
took it & wore it like the rhinestone broach my sisters refused /
I built myself in her image: her elaborate jheri curl her tight
gowns her refusal of anything waxing or waning away from
perfect & men & women who are lucky can keep our name in
their mouths at least until sunrise / I never caught that strong
man's name I never ask the right questions when the camera is
packed away / we held each other like wild trees growing too
close together / he said my name again & for the first time I
found myself thinking in silence / Ruby / he called out out & I
finally realized how lost I really was / chasing strange men
around even stranger forests while never catching anything not
even their name / only knowing they will call out for Ruby & I
will return.

Untitled
by Yoon Park

Still Light and Shine

by Jude Singer

No one had lived there for two or three years, the landlady said. But her placenta was buried in the front yard, under a slow-dying fig tree, and the baby who was once attached to the landlady through the placenta was born in the bathtub. The landlady was skinny and arguably brunette, the kind of Portland white lady that didn't dye her hair once it began to gray. She wore clogs, and clopped around the house giving them the tour.

Liz, barely a whisper behind Nim's shoulder, breathed, "Like a horse," into their ear.

The last people who lived here were Reed students, too. The landlady, Claudia, called them rowdy, noisy kids who'd trashed the place. Claudia said their names, which were all roughly masculine, generic. No one Nim knew. She showed them a mark in the wall where someone had thrown a metal water bottle and left an almost heart-shaped gouge in the plaster.

"A clown lives downstairs, in the basement unit," the landlady said, and the two of them, Liz and Nim, abruptly stopped walking, gathered together in a little bundle exchanging furtive looks. "She's in medical school. She's a good tenant, quiet."

Liz leaned into Nim's shoulder again, whispered, "A clown?" Nim said nothing, but gave her a gentle pinch on the wrist that might've meant *I don't know*, or *Keep walking*, or *Do something*.

The house came fully furnished and Nim's bedroom, the one on the first floor, had peacock feathers in vases. Liz's bedroom was upstairs and bubbling hot. There was a tiny closet, only half height, a crawl space that Liz could probably fit in if she took off her shoes and curled up like a shrimp. Across the hall from Liz, there was another door, closed. Claudia did not mention this, the third door.

The clown, who was, actually, studying for a doctorate in English literature, climbed up her stairs and into the shared backyard every morning, before Portland boiled over. Barefoot in the grass, she held four hula hoops in one hand, tossed them into the air like strange birds, caught each one on a foot or neck or elbow. There was no placenta in the backyard, but a raspberry bush, and a few old motorcycles that belonged to the landlady's husband, and a large pile of woodchips with a little sign that said "Not for sale".

The basement clown, who had a name that Nim nor Liz could ever seem to remember, gathered raspberries in a plastic bowl after she finished her hula hooping. They would congregate in Liz's bedroom, kneeling prostrate in front of the window, to look down upon this performance. The swinging hoops, wrapped in silvery tape, flashing in the light. The gathering of raspberries, the clown's elegant hand reaching out to pluck.

The clown was thirty-six and her dissertation was about the poetry of British women in the 1500s. She stood on one end of the long yard, greasy hair in a ponytail. Nim and Liz sat at the other end, in lawn chairs, huddled shyly.

"A lot of it is about sex," The clown said. "And motherhood." Nim nodded, as if this meant something to them. "And status. That type of woman, it was only women with status who could write poetry."

Every night, Liz gathered raspberries and they soaked them in wine that only Nim was old enough to purchase.

Liz studied religion and spent the first day walking around the house in socked feet, pointing out all the Buddhist symbols in this white home. Nim studied literature, which mostly meant that they didn't know what to study.

It was a summer when everything went quiet and so they both did fake jobs with fake titles while sitting on the couch in the meager air conditioning. On the nights when the air inside the house was hotter than outside, they sat on the stoop and smoked poorly rolled joints.

They spoke to no one else besides the clown and the land-lady, and, every once in a while, when he came to move one motorcycle onto a truck and leave a different motorcycle lean-ing in the backyard in its place, the landlady's husband. The husband would come without notice, which wasn't legal in Portland, but no one knew what to do about it, so no one did anything about it. He would knock on the door and ask to use the bathroom, and afterwards they would find that their things had been shuffled around, the caps on lotions slightly askew, the ghost of a thumbnail marring the smooth surface of a lip balm. This, too, no one knew what to do about. He had a soft face, vaguely shaped, so that Nim wasn't sure they would recognize him in a crowd. He never came when his wife was there. Nim knew that they probably should have been afraid of

the husband, but his face was so young and the disruption to lip balms and lotions so gentle, so inoffensive, that he seemed less frightening and more sad. Once, they found half a wood chip, from the pile in the yard that was not for sale, wedged in the skinny neck of Liz's shampoo.

The clown performed at children's birthday parties, but because this was a quiet summer no one's children had any birthday parties. The parties paid for the doctorate in English literature, but her true dream, the clown said, was to write a memoir. Sometimes, the clown would forget her keys in her car and leave it puffing exhaust into the front window of the up-stairs part of the house, the part that the clown did not live in, and Liz would be sent downstairs to knock on the clown's door.

Every single day was like the one before, stagnant air, gray sky, hot and green and wet. On a Monday, behind the door across from Liz's room, Liz heard scuttling. They took turns pressing ear, cheek, palm to the wood. And they agreed; inside, a scribbling sound, something or somethings with many legs moving around and around and around.

"Oh god," said Nim. "Oh, god. What do we do?"

Liz, because she did not know what to do, said, "Nothing.

We just wait."

The scuttling grew louder, and Liz noticed a liquid, slithering down the door as if the wood was weeping.

Many days Liz stood with her back against the door. Skin pressed to wood, she could tell that the inside was growing damper, that the something inside with the legs would soon be swimming. The water seeped under the cracks, even though she had duct taped the jamb. The carpet outside the door was already spongy. If she pressed her hand to the fibers, liquid bubbled up, a damp imprint of her fingers. She felt a certain responsibility for the second floor, because she felt it was hers to take care of and hers to sop up the water, but once the wet reached its fingers to Liz's bedroom, she called to Nim, showed them how to press their bare feet into the carpet and make the water surge around their toes.

Nim's joints were older than their body and soon the humidity from the Portland summer and from the door upstairs made their knees, hips lock stiff. They used a honey-based balm to

regain the bend of tissue and muscle, to mend the tears in their fascia. When Nim's joints hurt too much for the stairs, Liz would sit alone in her doorway and watch the water leak. The scuttling grew louder and sometimes beetles would wedge their way into the hall, like birth, like creation. They were fat beetles, glittery. Liz caught one to bring to Nim, marooned downstairs. Nim had dreams of the beetles crawling onto their face, their forehead, smoothing out the wrinkles. When the dream-beetles settled on their limbs, the creases where ball met socket, Nim would wake youthful again, the joint lubricated and slipping easily in and out of place.

When Nim was born the nurse broke their collarbone. It never knitted itself back quite right, so they'd sit and watch the door and rub the notch in their chest over and over again.

The clown turned thirty-seven and because it was a quiet summer only Nim and Liz were invited to the party. The clown performed a few verses of a poem by Katherine Philips who was some woman that was alive in a far away country during a far away century:

Then let our flames still light and shine, And no false fear control,

As innocent as our design, Immortal as our soul.

Nim and Liz clapped politely.

After she had finished the poem, the clown said:

"There's water dripping into my apartment."

Liz sucked in breath. "Is there?"

The clown did not respond, but smiled at Nim, at Liz, and the smile was tight, no teeth.

One morning Nim awoke and there was a beetle, prismed and material, perched on the crease of their hip bone.

The landlady's husband began to leave them notes in the bathroom, nothing frightening, just *"I like the painting above the bathtub, the one of the two ships in the ocean"*, *"It is so hot out today"*, *"I am worried about my motorcycles."* They hadn't seen him in days, but the notes

still came, on thin strips of notebook paper, curled up like messages in bottles, stacked tidily on the bathroom counter. Sometimes they were curved like love letters around one of the beetles, a carcass, lying dismal and dead in the sink.

Mold grew like fine mist on the ceilings, the notches where walls met. Saltwater dripped down the stairs, collected in a puddle at the base. The house became jungle, heat and steam and damp, bugs catching the light. They began to spread. Opaline chunks of insect on bedframes, on their clothes, in the sink and on the sofa and wedged inside the air conditioning unit. Liz and Nim could not bear to speak about the beetles, could only point, only gesture meaningfully when a bug came too close to eye or lip.

Liz awoke in her own bed, in her own room, an inch of water coating the floor and a beetle on each eyelid. In the way that the bathroom notes did not frighten her this did not frighten her, but she waded to Nim downstairs, a beetle in each hand, palms out, and said:

"We have to open the door."

Nim was eating an egg and turned their face away from the beetles in Liz's hand.

In the end they held hands and when a big wave like religion poured out, white rapids blustering around the stairs, they were not afraid. Beetles were caught up in the waves, flailing. Salt coated the shells of their ears. Ocean swam down the tall staircase, and when the first floor became interior lake, when the steps were half drowned, Liz and Nim on their knees shuffled to the doorway, made open.

Inside the door was a room. It was small and rotten, moss on the beams, and the landlady's husband stood in the center. He was hunched over his knees, chest to thigh, and he did not seem afraid, only wet, and tired. Fat insects like new quarters nestled in his hair.

He looked at them, and his face was kind and young, and he said, "I'm sorry. For this. I didn't mean for this to happen."

The clown's apartment had flooded and she had broken a window to escape from the basement and then broke a second window to climb into Nim's and Liz's house, and her hands

were bleeding but strong, made for swimming and plucking raspberries. She emerged from the sea and crawled up the stairs.

They were silent and they gathered here like this, the water draining, the beetles floating downstairs and out to the streets of Portland, to become wild in grass, to become outside in the way that Nim and Liz and the clown and the husband, in that quiet summer, could not become outside. And when each beetle had scurried out, when they had absolved themselves of their placement like jewelry on arms and hair, the clown reached her hand out and pulled the husband to his height. Her eyes were green and sad.

Nim stood up, then Liz, and they crept into this room, this cave, where there were no longer insects but leftover husks remained. They were not afraid but they were wet and tired, and they felt sorry for the husband. Nim said: "We forgive you."

Robot Learns to Write Poetry

by Valerie Hunter

It's a Thursday in November
when the robot spits out the poem.
Of course it's written poems before,
reams of them, but they were terrible,
full of silly rhymes and clichés
and bland, repetitious sentiments
like fourth-rate greeting cards.

But this poem is a masterpiece,
with crisp language and metaphors
that are deep without being arcane.
It can appeal to multiple generations,
be understood on multiple levels.
It doesn't rhyme, but it has a lovely
musicality that gets stuck in readers' heads,
invades their bloodstream, latches
onto their DNA and replicates.

To achieve this glorious poem,
the robot fed on the blood
of writers for months, consumed
three poet laureates
six popular lyricists,
and that girl on TikTok
who used to recite her poems
to millions of followers. Poetry
doesn't come easy, but the price
is worth it, or at least that's
what the algorithms say.
The public will be reprogrammed
until they agree wholeheartedly,
and can recite every word by heart.

Reading Summer
by Karen Lee

Summer: a sticky day that melts the old pages
off the flimsy, withering leather books
in the Lynchburg Public Library. A season where
the only refuge -
the air conditioned hallways.
Inside: a child scurries to the counter,
holding a pile of children's books,
lopsided and of a multitude of shapes and sizes. Like childrens'
books are.
The stack amounts above his head,
and he staggers to hold it straight.
The old woman by the counter brings up her glasses,
as if she cannot see the scene,
and sighs.
She does not move.
A smile decorates her lips as she enjoys the sight.
The background: playing Flight of the Bumblebee.
The child dances,
tiptoeing around the old wooden library.
The record keeps spinning.

Ash and Elm

by James Hall

Many have questioned,
in dream and in trance,
Whence the first woman, whence the first man,
Whence came the people, who live on this land?

Fated humans sprang from Ash and from Elm.
Hard and soft driftwood, of little worth,
tested by the older-gods at birth,
opposites joined, together ignite.

The Mother gave them the breath of life,
wisdom a gift from the tree of knowledge,
warmth and good health flowed from bright god Sun,
but the Wyrd carved their destiny.

Many have questioned,
in dream and in trance, from
whence comes the fire, whence come the flood?
Dark forces will stir when the moon shines blood.
Mountains tremble and glaciers melt,
a corpse-wind spreads across the land,
blown in on the wing of swans of death,
as the black wolf swallows the sun.

Many have questioned,
In dream and in trance,
After the Mighty-Winter is gone,
whom of the Iceir, if any, live on?

Life and Life-lover in garden dwell,
under Yggdrasil, beside Urd's well,
sustained by the fresh morning dew,
two now free of fate, to begin anew.

Quantum Physics
by Lynette G. Esposito

Everything I love is made of you
and me—
a world of complexity
where
we are entangled--
surrounded by
the uncertainty principle
that causes waves wherever
we are
as if we are made up of water
creatures
swimming blindly toward the horizon
with hope of getting there.

The Sixes
by Marianne Taylor

So there I was in the six
of swords, being ferried across
a dusky river to an uncertain

shore. Who was this child by my side?
And whose itchy cloak covered my head?
Sudden winds sprang up, drove us

downstream, brisk waves spitting,
spraying, knocking the six stiff
swords, one by one, out of

the boat and into the swirling depths.
The child clung to me, and the
ferryman swore, so I began

to sing about riding a proud
horse through a cheering crowd on a
blue sky day. My burgundy cloak

fell soft in folds, but a scratchy wreath
bothered my head, child now gone
from my grasp. Instead I held

in my right a stave, fist-bumped
revelers with my left. Soon to
arrive on a sunny hill, older,

heavier, bearing scales, slipping
coins into pale, thin hands. The earth
beneath my feet felt firm. Good

to be free of the horse and the boat.
And though the sky still blazed
blue, coins had changed to cups,

each filled with a flower. And you
stood beside me, young again
in the village where once we played.

You were the child after all.
And I loved you then, as I
love you now, wherever we are.

RADAGASTATOUILLE: THE LITTLE BROWN ISTARI'S LAMENT

by RJ Equality Ingram

a LOTR what if?

He came to us rolling barrels of spring water / riding one of the rolling barrels himself / & three others tied into a rigged catamaran pulled by the largest rabbits we've ever seen / parading down the road whistling a tune that smelled of elderflower & honey the rich ripe sound of holy bell blossoms ringing in a new child of Middle Earth / at least how it used to be done when he found us the guardians of the great long wilderness but we saw in him a goodness we had long forgotten / The travelers we do see often offer no respect in return for the spoils they take from us / But now we had a guardian who could protect us from the horrors that fall down the mountains / for a while we did that happily & suffering was nearly forgotten thanks to the man who rides sleds pulled by our neighbors who can out run a firecracker shot off by hobbits / from one of his adventures he brought home an artifact we are forbidden to name that swirls knowledge into destruction if disturbed or touched by the easily corrupted / but she was not corruptible my daughter when she pulled from the orb a single memory from the dark lords themselves / our friend the wizard knew the source of the world's rot was shifting which meant the time to recruit champions of the light was upon us! / But the darkness, my fellow travelers, listens even to those who shine the brightest & the orb retaliated & shot at my daughter our princess / a vision so painful that when it hit the wizard's chest as he intercepted Radagast The Brown saw all the world's pain at once & it curdled him into smithereens but luckily his heart was hit & not his mind / his mind remains controllable if my daughter can maintain the right level of concentration.

BIOS

AEESHA ABDULLAHI ALHAJI
Aeesha Abdullahi Alhaji is a poet and a creative writer whose works have appeared/forthcoming on the Chiron Review, Blue Minaret Journal, Crank Magazine, The Yellow House, The Beatnikcowboy, Tampered Press Journal, ParABnormal Magazine, The Open Collective Magazine and elsewhere. She is a member of the Hilltop Creative Arts Foundation, Minna Literary Society and has received a fellowship from the Ebedi International Writer's Residency. She tweets @AlhajiAeesha on X(Formerly Twitter).

PHILIP ATHANS
Editor and author Philip Athans has been a driving force behind varied media including Alternative fiction & poetry magazine and Wizards of the Coast. He lives and works in the Pacific Northwest.

LINDSAY BAIK
Lindsay Baik is a student at an international school in Seoul who is passionate about writing, art, and collecting CDs. She spends much of her free time playing the guitar and listening to music. Currently, Lindsay is working on building her portfolio.

ANNA CLASSON
 I am a junior at Kutztown University majoring in Professional Writing.

MICKEY COLLINS
Mickey ~~rights wrongs~~. Mickey ~~wrongs rites~~. Mickey writes words, sometimes wrong words but he tries to get it write.

TINAMARIE COX
Tinamarie Cox lives in Arizona with her husband, two children, and a one-eyed cat. Her written and visual work has appeared in numerous publications in a variety of genres. You can find more of her work on Instagram @tinamariethinkstoomuch and her website tinamariethinkstoomuch.weebly.com.

LYNETTE ESPOSITO
Lynette G. Esposito, MA Rutgers, has been published in *Poetry Quarterly*, *North of Oxford*, *Twin Decades*, *Remembered Arts*, *Reader's Digest*, *US1*, and others. She was married to Attilio Esposito and lives with eight rescued muses in Southern New Jersey.

Robert Eversmann
Robert Eversmann works for *Deep Overstock*.

Sarah Das Gupta
Sarah Das Gupta is a retired English teacher from near Cambridge, UK. She taught in India, Tanzania as well as the UK. As the head of department, she was often charged with overseeing the English section of the School Library and purchasing books.In most schools she was also responsible for stocking class libraries. She started writing this year after an accident which kept her in hospital. Her work has been published in many magazines from twelve countries, including US, UK, Australia, Canada, India, Germany, Croatia and Romania. Writing has given her the challenge and drive to learn to walk again.

John Grey
John Grey is an Australian poet, US resident, recently published in New World Writing, North Dakota Quarterly and Lost Pilots. Latest books, "Between Two Fires", "Covert" and "Memory Outside The Head" are available through Amazon. Work upcoming in California Quarterly, Birmingham Arts Journal, La Presa and Soul Ink. I have spent a lifetime as a curator of my own library which has historically contained more books than I will ever hope to read.

James Hall
James Hall's poetry collection Prairie Roots was published April 2023 by Shanti Arts Publishing. His writing has appeared in Hobo Camp Review, Utopia, Deep Overstock, and others. He is a writer and physician with interests in cider craft, cross country skiing and dire portents.

Heather Hambley
Heather is a Latin teacher turned translator. She has a BA in Classics from Reed College, where she developed a passion for prose composition and mythological women. She lives in Central Oregon with her husband Andy and their senior poodle Mo. She loves watching scary movies and curates feel-good horror sets at happyspookies.substack.com.

Tom Holmes
For twenty-two years, Tom Holmes was the founding editor and curator of Redactions: Poetry & Poetics. Holmes is also the author of five full-length collections of poetry, including The Book of Incurable Dreams (Xavier Review Press) and The Cave, which won The Bitter Oleander Press Library of Poetry Book Award for 2013, as well as four chapbooks. He teaches at

Nashville State Community College (Clarksville). His writings about wine, poetry book reviews, and poetry can be found at his blog, The Line Break: thelinebreak.wordpress.com/. Follow him on Twitter: @TheLineBreak

VALERIE HUNTER
Valerie Hunter worked at her college library as an undergrad, where she occasionally read the new acquisitions when she should have been shelving. She now teaches high school English and maintains a classroom library with a sadly low circulation rate. Her poems have appeared in publications including *Room Magazine*, *Wizards in Space*, and *Frost Meadow Review*.

RJ EQUALITY INGRAM
RJ Equality Ingram works as a used bookseller for Goodwill Industries of the Collumbia Willamette. Their first collection of poetry *The Autobiography of Nancy Drew* is forthcoming from White Stag Publishing in early 2024. RJ received their MFA in creative writing from Saint Mary's College of California with concentrations in poetry & creative nonfiction. More work can be found in *Phoebe Journal*, *Miniskirt Magazine* & *Citron Review* among others. RJ's cat Brenda lost a leg designing her memory palace.

ALETHA IRBY
My name is Aletha Irby and I have been writing poetry for over fifty years. My personal library includes books of poetry, mysteries, ghost stories, novels, and histories. My work has been published in *Main Street Rag*, *Lady Blue Literary Arts Journal*, *VOLT*, *Shot Glass Journal*, *Palo Alto Review*, *Tiny Lights Online*, and many other journals. I am very grateful to have been granted this time, on this planet, to spend with the English language.

RYAN KIM
Ryan Kim is a high school art student based in South Korea. Drawing inspiration from his cultural heritage and the dynamic environment of his surroundings, Ryan explores themes of identity, tradition, and modernity through his artwork. With a keen eye for detail and a passion for storytelling, he seeks to provoke thought and evoke emotion in his audience. He aspires to continue his artistic journey, sharing his unique perspective with audiences worldwide.

SEUNGMIN KIM
Seungmin Kim is a diligent scholar enrolled at the Hong Kong International School. Presently, he is meticulously curating his compilation of written works with the aim of fortifying his candidacy for admission to esteemed academic institutions.

Sigrid Kim

Sigrid Kim is a student attending a high school in Virginia, where she actively engages in writing, drawing, and caring for her two beloved dogs, Oliver and Cooper. In preparation for her future academic endeavors, she is currently assembling her portfolio and has recently secured admission to Juniper's Young Writers Camp and Sewanee.

Sean Kyung

Sean Kyung is currently attending an international school in the vibrant city of Seoul, South Korea. His ardent pursuit lies in creating an impressive art portfolio for university admissions.

Grace Lee

Grace Lee, a high school student in Seoul, South Korea, is passionate about words. Whether crafting stories or poems, she blends her unique perspective with the vibrant culture of Seoul. Excited to contribute to the literary landscape, Grace's writing reflects the universal themes of adolescence in a big city.

Karen Lee

Karen Lee is a student at Chadwick International in Seoul, South Korea, who has an unquenchable passion for both writing and drawing. In preparation for her future academic endeavors, she is diligently compiling her writing portfolio and has recently received an acceptance to Iowa Young Writer's Studio, a distinguished program that identifies and nurtures emerging writing tale.

Tk Tekkyu Lee

Tk Tekkyu Lee is meticulously assembling his art portfolio. His work showcases a fusion of traditional and contemporary techniques. Each piece in his portfolio tells a captivating story, drawing viewers into his imaginative world. Tk is a student in the world of emerging young artists, and his portfolio is a testament to his dedication and creative prowess.

Timothy Arliss OBrien

Timothy Arliss OBrien (he/they) is an interdisciplinary artist in music composition, writing, and visual art. He has premiered music from opera to film scores to electronic ambient projects. He has published several books of poetry, (*The Queer Revolt, The Art of Learning to Fly, & Happy LGBTQ Wrath Month*), and is a poetry editor for *Deep Overstock*, a judge for Reedsy Prompts, and a poetry reader for *Okay Donkey*. He also founded the podcast & small press publishing house, The Poet Heroic, and the digital magic space

The Healers Coven. He also showcases his psychedelic makeup skills as the phenomenal drag queen Tabitha Acidz.
Check out more at his website: www.timothyarlissobrien.com

Jahin Claire Oh
Jahin Claire Oh is a tenth grader attending a high school in San Jose, California. She likes to code and takes an interest in media art for fun. She prefers warm tones over cool tones and generally likes calming imagery with naturalistic depictions. In her free time, she likes to spend time with her friends and occasionally goes to local art exhibits.

Brian Park
Brian Park is a ninth-grade student attending high school in Massachusetts with a passion for visual arts. Brian's art portfolio encompasses a range of mediums and styles, reflecting his diverse interests and inspirations. Outside of his artistic pursuits, Brian enjoys exploring nature, reading, and spending time with friends and family. He is excited about the possibility of sharing his artwork with a wider audience and looks forward to continuing to grow as an artist.

Yoon Park
Yoon Park is a dynamic high school student enrolled at an international school in Seoul, South Korea. She channels her creative energy into writing and visual art and finds joy in expressing herself through these mediums. Additionally, she has a passion for music and spends her spare time playing the piano or the guitar. Her dedication to her craft has earned her recognition and admission into the prestigious Sewanee Young Writers Conference.

Jihye Shin
Jihye Shin is a Korean-American poet and bookseller based in Florida.

Jude Singer
Jude Singer is a fiction writer and poet living in Portland, Oregon. He writes about being transgender, having a body, experiencing grief, and strange weather patterns. He was a 2022 finalist for the New York Time's Modern Love College Essay contest.

Marianne Taylor
Marianne Taylor is a bookseller at Powell's on Burnside where she manages the sales floor in the Blue, Gold, and Green rooms. In a previous life she taught literature and creative writing at a Midwestern college, and her poetry has been published widely in national journals and anthologies. She once

served as Poet Laureate of her former small town, but for the past three years she's been trying to find her way around Portland.

Z.B. Wagman

Z.B. Wagman is an editor for the *Deep Overstock Literary Journal* and a co-host of the Deep Overstock Fiction podcast. When not writing or editing he can be found behind the desk at the Beaverton City Library, where he finds much inspiration.

Nicholas Yandell

Nicholas Yandell is a composer, who sometimes creates with words instead of sound. In those cases, he usually ends up with fiction and occasionally poetry. He also paints and draws, and often all these activities become combined, because they're really not all that different from each other, and it's all just art right?
When not working on creative projects, Nick works as a bookseller at Powell's Books in Portland, Oregon, where he enjoys being surrounded by a wealth of knowledge, as well as working and interacting with creatively stimulating people. He has a website where he displays his creations; it's nicholasyandell.com. Check it out!